This Little Tiger book belongs to:

_____

_____

_____

_____

For Sue and Paul
- A.H.B.

For Jess
- T.W.

LITTLE TIGER PRESS
1 The Coda Centre, 189 Munster Road,
London SW6 6AW
www.littletiger.co.uk
First published in Great Britain 1998
by Little Tiger Press, London
This edition published 2013
Text copyright © A.H. Benjamin 1998
Illustrations copyright © Tim Warnes 1998
A.H. Benjamin and Tim Warnes have asserted
their rights to be identified as the author and
illustrator of this work under the Copyright,
Designs and Patents Act, 1988
All rights reserved • ISBN 978-1-84895-794-7
Printed in China • LTP/1900/0735/0713
10 9 8 7 6 5 4 3 2

IT COULD HAVE
BEEN WORSE

A.H. Benjamin　　　　**Tim Warnes**

LITTLE TIGER PRESS

Mouse was on his way back home after
visiting his town cousin when . . .

WHOOPS!

. . . he lost his balance and fell to the ground.

"Ouch!" said Mouse.
"This isn't my
lucky day."

But it could have
been worse!

Mouse picked himself up
and continued on his way.
He came to an open field
and was scurrying across it
when . . .

CRASH!

. . . he fell into a dark hole.

"Why do things always go wrong for me?" grumbled Mouse.

But it could have been worse!

Mouse climbed out of the hole and
was off again, but soon he got sleepy.

"I think I'll take a rest," Mouse said.
He had just found a comfortable spot when . . .

OUCH!

. . . he sat on a thistle
and shot into the air.

"Everything bad happens to me!" wailed Mouse, as he pulled the thorns out of his fur.

But it could have been worse!

Mouse trotted down the hill until he reached a stream. He began to cross it using the stepping stones when . . .

"I'll catch a cold!"
complained Mouse.

But it could have been worse!

Mouse paddled to the edge of the
stream and climbed out of the water.

Shaking himself dry, he was just about to scramble down a steep bank when . . .

WHEEE!

. . . he lost his footing and
skidded to the bottom.

"I'll be black and blue all over," cried Mouse.

But it could have been worse!

Mouse staggered to his feet and ran the rest of the way home.

"It's been a terrible day," he said to his mother as she bathed his cuts and bruises. "I fell into a hole, got wet in the river, and—" "Never mind, son," she said . . .